MW00955432

# Table of Contents

Rourke
Educational Media

*A Division of*
Carson Dellosa Education

rourkeeducationalmedia.com

# Can you find these words?

## basket

## church

## eggs

## lambs

# We Celebrate Easter!

**Easter comes in the spring.**

# Let's see baby animals.

**Lambs** are born in spring.

Easter is a holy day for Christians.

Eggs stand for new life.

Let's fill a **basket!**

basket

# Let's eat candy!

Bite into jelly beans and chocolate treats.

# Did you find these words?

Let's fill a **basket!**

Let's go to **church**.

Let's hunt for **eggs**.

**Lambs** are born in spring.

# Photo Glossary

 **basket** (BAS-kit): A container with handles.

 **church** (church): A building used for worshipping a god.

 **eggs** (egs): Round or oval objects laid by birds, fish, insects, or reptiles.

 **lambs** (lams): Baby sheep.

# Index

# About the Author

Lisa Jackson is a writer from Columbus, Ohio. She likes to ride her bike and collect pennies. Her favorite holiday is the one that is coming up next!

© 2020 Rourke Educational Media

All rights reserved. No part of this book may be reproduced or utilized in any form or by any means, electronic or mechanical including photocopying, recording, or by any information storage and retrieval system without permission in writing from the publisher.

www.rourkeeducationalmedia.com

PHOTO CREDITS: Cover: ©By Anneka; Pg 2, 5, 14, 15 ©By Michal Pesata; Pg 2, 10, 14, 15 ©RomoloTavani; Pg 2, 6, 14, 15 ©leightrail; Pg 2, 8, 14, 15 ©AleksandarNakic; Pg 3 ©Moncherie; Pg 4 ©By Santirat Praeknokkaew; Pg 7 ©By Rawpixel.com; Pg 12 ©bhofack2; Pg 13 ©By Pixel Prose Images

Edited by: Keli Sipperley

Cover and interior design by: Kathy Walsh

**Library of Congress PCN Data**

Easter / Lisa Jackson

(Holidays Around the World)

ISBN 978-1-73160-577-1 (hard cover)(alk. paper)

ISBN 978-1-73160-452-1 (soft cover)

ISBN 978-1-73160-626-6 (e-Book)

ISBN 978-1-73160-689-1 (ePub)

Library of Congress Control Number: 2018967334

Printed in the United States of America,

North Mankato, Minnesota